CELEBRATE
HOLIDAYS

Celebrate Columbus Day

Joanne Mattern

Schoolchildren ride in a replica of one of Columbus's three
ships during the Columbus Day parade in New York City.

Enslow Publishers, Inc.
40 Industrial Road
Box 398
Berkeley Heights, NJ 07922
USA
    http://www.enslow.com

Library of Congress Cataloging-in-Publication Data

Mattern, Joanne, 1963–
    Celebrate Columbus Day / Joanne Mattern.
        p. cm. — (Celebrate holidays)
    Includes bibliographical references and index.
    ISBN 0-7660-2580-2
        1. Columbus Day—Juvenile literature. 2. Columbus, Christopher—Juvenile literature. 3. America—Discovery and exploration—Spanish—Juvenile literature. I. Title. II. Series.
    E120.M38 2006
    394.264—dc22
                                        2005028108

Printed in the United States of America

10 9 8 7 6 5 4 3 2 1

To Our Readers: We have done our best to make sure all Internet Addresses in this book were active and appropriate when we went to press. However, the author and the publisher have no control over and assume no liability for the material available on those Internet sites or on other Web sites they may link to. Any comments or suggestions can be sent by e-mail to comments@ enslow.com or to the address on the back cover.

Every effort has been made to locate all copyright holders of material used in this book. If any errors or omissions have occurred, corrections will be made in future editions of this book.

Illustration Credits: © 1999 Artville, LLC, pp. 10, 14, 22, 37, 39 (map); Associated Press, pp. 1, 62, 64, 67, 69, 70, 73, 74, 76, 83, 85; Corel Corporation, pp. 12, 18, 47, 52; © 2005 JupiterImages, p. 20; © 2006 JupiterImages, pp. 5, 11, 29, 43, 44, 48, 53, 54, 55, 57, 65, 71, 77, 88 (both), 89 (both); Library of Congress, pp. 4, 7, 8, 24, 27, 32, 35, 39 (portrait), 42, 72 (all three), 79; Photodisc, p. 58.

Cover Illustration: Associated Press.

CONTENTS

After a month on the open sea, Columbus's crew was restless as the search for Asia continued.

Land!

The sailors on board the three ships were getting restless. They had left Spain on August 3 and had their last sight of land after they left the Canary Islands on September 9. Now, more than two weeks later, the men wondered if the vast ocean stretching all around them would ever end.

Even though his crew was nervous and angry, the commander of the voyage was not worried. Christopher Columbus had studied maps before he and his crew left Spain. He knew that the ocean did not go on forever. He was sure that soon his ships, the *Niña*, the *Pinta*, and the *Santa María* would reach Asia. Columbus wanted to show everyone that explorers could reach the riches of Asia by sailing west around the world.

On September 25, Martín Pinzon, the captain of the *Pinta*, thought he saw land. The sailors climbed the ships' masts and thought they saw land too. However, they were mistaken. The journey continued.[1]

There were more false alarms. Finally, on October 12, 1492, at 2:00 in the morning, a sailor named Juan Rodriguez Bermejo got the first sight of what everyone had been waiting for. Standing in the front of the *Pinta* and staring across the water in the bright moonlight, Bermejo saw a line of low, white cliffs. "Tierra! Tierra!" he called in Spanish. "Land! Land!"[2] Finally, Columbus and his sailors had reached their goal.

The next morning, Columbus and his crew got their first look at the natives of this place. Columbus was startled to see that the inhabitants were naked and assumed that they were poor and uncivilized. Columbus was determined to get along with these natives. He wrote in his journal, "In order that they would be friendly toward us . . . to

The men finally spotted land, got into a small boat, and rowed ashore.

some of them I gave red caps, and glass beads which they put on their chests, and many other things of small value, in which they took so much pleasure and became so much our friends that it was a marvel."[3] The natives returned the gesture later, when several swam out to Columbus's ships. They brought gifts including parrots, cotton thread, and weapons.

The Taíno brought small treasures to Columbus and his men.

At first, Columbus enjoyed meeting and studying these natives. However, as the days passed, he began to wonder if he had really achieved what he had set out to do. Columbus's goal was to land in Asia, a land filled with jewels, spices, and other riches. Like others of his day, he believed the world had only three continents: Europe, Asia, and Africa.[4] Columbus believed he had reached Asia and was puzzled when his meetings with natives and his explorations of the islands revealed none of the gold and other riches he had expected to find.

Today we know that Columbus did not land in Asia. Instead, he landed on an island in the Bahamas, near the shores of North America and South America. Columbus did not find the riches he had dreamed of. He did not find the short route to Asia he had imagined either. Columbus did much more than that. He revealed the existence of a whole new world to the Europeans. Although Columbus never landed on the mainland of either North or South America, he changed the course of American history and culture on both continents.

Western Europe

Christoper Columbus was born in Italy and later traveled to Spain and Portugal.

ICELAND

Norwegian Sea

NORWAY

SWEDEN

FINLAND

SCOTLAND

DENMARK

IRELAND

ENGLAND

NETHERLANDS

Atlantic Ocean

BELGIUM   GERMANY

LUXEMBOURG

FRANCE

SWITZERLAND   AUSTRIA

PORTUGAL   SPAIN   ITALY

GREECE

Mediterranean Sea

The Life of Christopher Columbus

One of the most famous men in American history was not American at all. And though Christopher Columbus won fame and fortune as an explorer for Spain, he was not Spanish either. Columbus was actually Italian. Even more surprising, we know very little about the man who brought about what the Spanish historian Francisco Lopez de Gomara called in 1552 "the greatest event since the creation of the world."[1]

Genoa, Italy, looks like this today.

Christopher Columbus was born in the late summer or early fall of 1451 in Genoa, Italy. He was the first child of weavers Domenico and Susanna Colombo. They named their new son Cristoforo. Cristoforo would eventually have three younger brothers and a younger sister.

Genoa was an important seaport, and the city was filled with boats arriving and leaving for ports all over Europe. Cristoforo loved boats and wanted nothing more than to sail on one. However, his childhood was filled with work in his parents' weaving business. He never went to school and did not learn to read or write until he was an adult.[2]

The Indies

Two parts of the world are known as the Indies. The East Indies are located in Asia. They include India, Pakistan, Bangladesh, Myanmar, Sri Lanka, Thailand, Malaysia, Indonesia, Brunei, the Philippines, Singapore, and other nearby areas. The nations of the Caribbean are called the West Indies. These countries received their name because Christopher Columbus thought he was in the Indies when he landed in Hispaniola. To avoid confusion, the term West Indies was given to this part of the world to set it apart from the East Indies.

European nations began exploring the East Indies during the late fifteenth and early sixteenth centuries. Portugal and Spain had the most active explorers. The Indies were filled with spices, cloth, jewels, and other goods that were rare or unknown in Europe. These treasures led the Indies to become an important trading partner with Europe.

Just as the West Indies and other areas of the New World were colonized by European nations, the East Indies were colonized by Europeans too. India was controlled by Great Britain until 1948. The Philippines were ruled by the Spanish, and the Netherlands controlled much of Indonesia.[3]

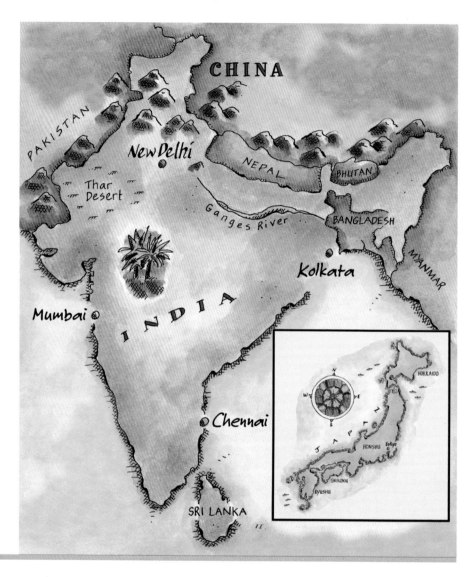

During Columbus's time, people called the countries of India, China, and Japan the Indies. This is what the map looks like today.

Cristoforo's dreams of going to sea came true when he was about fourteen years old. Historians think that his father sent Cristoforo on journeys along the coast of the Mediterranean Sea to sell cloth and buy wool in the towns along the water. Along with his work in the family business, Cristoforo studied sailing. By the time he was an adult, he knew how to steer, work the ship's sails, and navigate. He was ready to make a living as a sailor.

On one of Columbus's first voyages, he landed in Lisbon, Portugal. His brother and many other people from Genoa lived there. Portugal was also the center of exploration. The government paid many ship captains and sailors to explore the oceans. Their main goal was to find a shorter route to China and the Indies in the Far East.

During the 1400s, Europe was divided into many nations and city-states. There was a lot of competition between these nations and city-states, and governments were always trying to make their empires bigger. In addition, merchants were important people in most countries. Their goal was to acquire wealth by buying and selling goods. The key to acquiring wealth was trading with other lands that had riches not found in Europe. Most of those lands lay to the east, on the continent of Asia.

Europe had long viewed Asia as "a treasure house, a place of rare and wonderful things."[4] Asia was filled with goods that could make the merchants of Europe rich: spices, jewels, gold, copper, perfumes, silk, and much more. However, reaching Asia by land was long and difficult. Travelers faced geographic barriers, such as mountains. There were political obstacles too. Turkey and the other nations that made up the Middle East were often at war with each other and with European nations. Religious differences between the Christian Europeans and Muslim Arabs of the Middle East made things worse. For a time, it was acceptable for Muslims to trade with Europeans, even though they were considered infidels. However, by the mid-1400s, that attitude had changed, making it unsafe to travel through this part of the globe.[5] Nations such as Portugal, Spain, and the city-states of Genoa and Venice began looking for other ways to reach the riches of the Far East.

Meanwhile, Columbus had settled in Lisbon, Portugal. He felt at home there and began learning all he could about exploring. He worked with his brother making maps and taught himself to read and write in Spanish and Portuguese. He read any book he could find about geography.

The Importance of Spices

Spices were a vital part of life for wealthy Europeans who lived hundreds of years ago. Explorers sought new trading routes to get spices from the Far East back to Europe. Without the reward of finding spices, the exploration of the world might have taken much longer!

Spices were important because they added flavor to food. During the Middle Ages, there was no such thing as refrigeration. The quality of meat also was not very good. To keep meat from spoiling, it had to be smoked or preserved. This often led to tough, chewy meals without much flavor.

Spices were usually used in food, but people discovered other uses for them as well. Cinnamon could be used in drugs, oils, perfume, and cosmetics. Pepper could also be used as medicine, and also repelled insects. In time, spices became so valuable that they were used as money. Debts were paid with spices rather than gold or silver.[6]

People wanted to find Asia because of the popular spices that were used to hide the taste of spoiled food.

Columbus also fell in love. In 1479, he married a woman named Felipa. Felipa's father had been a sea captain and explorer who had discovered the Madeiras Islands off the coast of Africa. Columbus and his wife moved to the Madeiras and lived there for several years with their son, Diego. Columbus continued to sail. However, he was becoming more interested in exploring new lands rather than sailing to places everyone already knew about.

At that time, the Atlantic Ocean was called the Ocean Sea. No one knew how big it was. Columbus studied maps and did many calculations. He decided that a skilled sailor such as himself could sail across the Ocean Sea and reach the Far East. Columbus knew that many Portuguese explorers had found new lands and discovered great riches by sailing south. He believed he could find land by sailing west.[7]

Columbus was not the only person to feel this way. Between 1273 and 1293, an Italian merchant named Marco Polo lived and traveled in the Far East. When he finally returned to Venice, he wrote about his travels in a book called *Description of the World*. In the book, Marco Polo calculated the size of Asia. His measurements were wrong and made Asia much larger than it actually is, but no one knew that at the time.[8] Later, Columbus and other scholars used these measurements to calculate what the distance between Europe and Asia would be if a person traveled west across the Ocean Sea.

Two of the scholars who worked on these calculations were Paolo Toscanelli, an Italian physician who had studied maps, and Fernao Martins, a Portuguese churchman. In a letter to Martins in 1474, Toscanelli created a chart showing that only 5,000 miles (8,045 kilometers) separated Portugal and China. His chart also included islands along the way. Toscanelli noted that on this journey there were "no great spaces of the sea to be passed."[9] Columbus and Toscanelli later exchanged letters, and Toscanelli encouraged the younger man's plan to reach Asia by sailing west.

Marco Polo

In 1484, Columbus and his family moved back to Lisbon. Columbus brought his idea for reaching Asia to King John II and asked the Portuguese king to provide the ships and supplies Columbus needed to sail across the Ocean Sea. The king said no. He did not believe Columbus's calculations

Marco Polo

Marco Polo was born in 1254, in Venice, Italy. His father and uncle were wealthy merchants who traded with some Eastern cities. In 1271, seventeen-year-old Marco went with his father and uncle to visit to the Grand Khan Kublai, also called Kublai Khan. Kublai Khan was the ruler of the Mongolian empire in Beijing, China. Marco became a good friend of Kublai Khan and worked for the ruler for almost twenty years. He finally left China in 1291. After other journeys through the East, Marco returned to Venice in 1295.

A few years later, Venice went to war against another Italian city, Genoa. Marco was captured and imprisoned for several months. During this time, Marco wrote a book about his journeys in the East. The book was called *Description of the World*, but was commonly called *Il milione*.

After Marco was released, he went back to live and work with his father and uncle. He married and had several children. Although Marco was wealthy and well-respected, some people still did not believe his amazing stories. Before his death in 1324, a priest asked Marco to confess that he had lied. Marco refused and said, "I have not told half of what I saw."[10]

Christopher Columbus went from Italy to Portugal.

that most of the earth was made up of three landmasses separated by small areas of ocean. Neither did a panel of advisors he consulted. They all agreed that Columbus's geography was in error and his request should be turned down. King John was also annoyed by Columbus's arrogant personality. The Portuguese historian Joao de Barros wrote that "The King, as he observed this

Cristovao Colom [sic] to be a big talker and boastful in setting forth his accomplishments, and full of fancy and imagination . . . gave him small credit."[11]

Then something even worse happened. Columbus's wife died. Heartbroken, Columbus and his son moved to Spain to start a new life. Columbus married a Spanish woman named Beatriz, and the couple had a son, Ferdinand.

In Spain, Columbus looked for someone to sponsor his voyage. He became friends with Fray Antonio de Marchena, an important member of the Franciscan order of priests. Columbus met Fray Antonio when he enrolled his son Diego in a Franciscan school. Fray Antonio was very interested in exploration and was well known at the Spanish royal court. He suggested that Columbus bring his ideas to Don Enrique de Guzman, the Duke of Medina Sidonia and the wealthiest man in Spain.[12] The duke thought Columbus's idea was a good one and presented it to the Spanish king and queen. However, King Ferdinand and Queen Isabella thought the duke's presentation was too arrogant and turned him down.[13]

Next, Columbus told his idea to Don Luis de la Cerda, the Duke of Medina-Celi. The Duke gave Columbus a letter introducing him to the Spanish court, and Queen Isabella replied that Columbus should come see her.[14] Columbus did just that early in 1486.

King Ferdinand and Queen Isabella of Spain were happy to meet the determined explorer. Queen Isabella liked Columbus and his idea of finding a shortcut to the Far East. She asked a group of advisors to study his proposal and meet

The king and queen's advisors did not like Columbus's ideas and turned their back to him.

with Columbus. Several years later, the advisors said no. They believed that Columbus's calculations were wrong and the Ocean Sea was much wider than the explorer thought. However, Queen Isabella was still intrigued by Columbus's idea. She suggested that he bring his case to court at a later date.

Columbus was disappointed, but he was not ready to give up. He met with the king and queen and their financial advisors again in 1491. At first, the royals and their committee were put off by Columbus's demands. He wanted to be granted the title "Admiral of the Ocean Sea." He wanted to be governor of any new lands he claimed for Spain. He also demanded 10 percent of all the riches Spain got from these lands. Columbus's claims were too much. Once again, he was turned down.[15]

However, Columbus had impressed several members of the Spanish court. One of them was Luis de Santangel. He controlled part of the royal treasury. He argued with the king and queen about their decision. Santangel insisted that it would cost Spain nothing to give Columbus the titles he wanted. He also said that if another ruler sponsored Columbus's voyage and he was successful, "it would clearly be a great injury to [Isabella's] estate and a cause of just reproach by

King Ferdinand and Queen Isabella

King Ferdinand and Queen Isabella were the first rulers of a united Spain. Isabella I of Castile was born in 1451. Ferdinand II of Aragon was born in 1452. Castile and Aragon were two powerful Spanish kingdoms. The two married in 1469. After Isabella's brother died in 1474, Isabella and Ferdinand both ascended to the throne. Because their union brought Castile and Aragon together, they became rulers of a united Spain.[16]

Ferdinand and Isabella were called "los Reyes Catolicos," or "the Catholic Monarchs." Their reign was closely tied to the Catholic Church. Although they are probably best remembered for sponsoring Christopher Columbus's voyage to the New World, which brought great wealth and power to Spain, Ferdinand and Isabella's reign had a darker side. They started the Spanish Inquisition, a vicious campaign against non-Christians, and were also responsible for expelling Jews from Spain. Isabella died in 1504, and Ferdinand died in 1516.[17]

her friends and of censure by her enemies."[18] In other words, Queen Isabella would look foolish and everyone would think less of her. This appeal to the queen's pride worked. After giving the matter more thought, Isabella and Ferdinand agreed to pay for Columbus's voyage.

Columbus spent many months preparing for his journey. Finally, he left Palos, Spain, on August 3, 1492. He had a crew of about ninety men and three ships called the *Niña*, the *Pinta*, and the *Santa María*. The ships stopped at the Canary

King Ferdinand and Queen Isabella of Spain were eager to meet the determined explorer.

Islands off the coast of Africa to pick up supplies and make repairs. Then, on September 9, they set off across the vast expanse of the ocean.

Columbus kept a journal of each day's sailing. He noted how far they had sailed, what the weather was like, and other specific details. Columbus also described life on board ship. This life was not easy. Most of the space below decks was taken up by food, water, firewood, gunpowder, and other supplies for the journey. This meant that the sailors had to sleep up on the deck. If bad weather forced them below, they had to squeeze into the tiny, cramped spaces between the supplies. The sailors did not have beds or pillows, yet the work of sailing a ship was so exhausting that they probably did not have any trouble falling asleep. However, Columbus, the other ships' captains, and perhaps their pilots would have had covered spaces in which to sleep.[19] Sailors ate one hot meal a day and lived mostly on a type of biscuit called hardtack, as well as salted beef, pork, and any fish they caught while at sea.

A sailor's day was divided into four-hour shifts called watches. The men did the work of sailing the ship and keeping everything repaired and in good shape. They also kept watch for storms, other ships, and, of course, any sight of land. The day

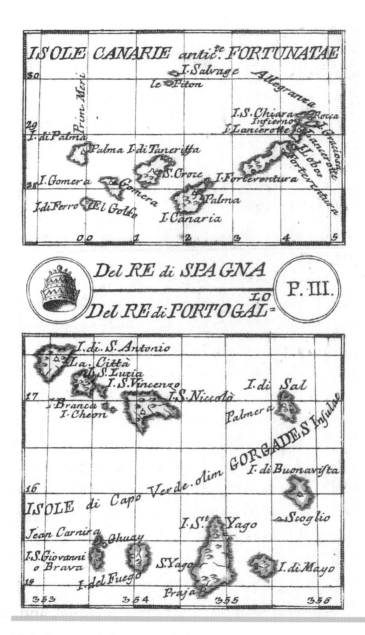

This is an old map of the Canary Islands.

also included religious observances. There was no priest on board any of Columbus's ships, but Columbus read prayers to his men at certain hours of the day. These prayers provided a comforting rhythm to the hard work of sailing across the ocean.[20]

Columbus navigated by a method called dead reckoning. At night, keeping the North Star in view also helped the men to continue sailing west. Columbus also factored in the trade winds that

Dead Reckoning

Dead reckoning is a way to estimate where you are based on where you were at a previous time. Before modern navigational methods were available, dead reckoning was one way explorers and other travelers charted their course across the ocean.

To use dead reckoning, a navigator takes the boat's last known position. This position is called the fix. Then he figures out the fix interval. The fix interval is how long it will take to get to the next known position and is calculated by looking at the ship's speed, time, and direction. By figuring out how long it should take for a ship to get from one point to another, a navigator can estimate where the ship is at any given moment.

blew across the Ocean Sea. Because these winds blow toward the northeast, Columbus knew he had to sail southwest in order to stay on course. If he had tried to sail due west, the winds would have pushed him too far north to follow the route he had laid out.[21]

Columbus and his men had good weather for most of their trip. They were able to cover nearly 850 miles between September 9 and September 16.[22] On September 18, Martín Pinzon, the captain of the *Pinta*, told Columbus that he had sighted land the night before. Columbus assumed Pinzon had seen small islands that many people of the time believed existed in the Ocean Sea. Instead of looking for them, Columbus continued his westerly course. The ships traveled through the Sargasso Sea, an area of thick, floating seaweed in the ocean, and saw many birds and whales.

Although the journey was going well, the men began to get restless as the days passed with no sign of land. There were even rumors that some of the sailors wanted to throw Columbus overboard.[23] The farther they sailed, the more worried the sailors became. Although the people of that time knew the world was round and that it was impossible to fall off the edge, the crew had plenty of other things to worry about. Would they run into sea monsters? Would the voyage ever end, or would they be lost at sea forever? Columbus, however, remained calm and sure of himself. His patience was rewarded in the early days of October when Columbus and his crew saw large flocks of birds flying west. They knew this was a sign that land was near.

In spite of the birds, the men were still doubtful that they would ever reach land. Columbus wrote in his journal that he "reproached them for their lack of spirit."[24] He convinced his men to keep the faith by appealing to their sense of duty and promising them a share in the riches they would find. Finally, the crew agreed to sail on for three more days. If they had not spotted land by that time, Columbus agreed he would turn back.[25]

During Columbus's time, many people thought there were sea monsters in the oceans.

Taíno

The Taíno were indigenous, or native, people who lived in the Caribbean islands at the time Columbus journeyed to that part of the world. The Taíno lived in what are now the Bahamas, Cuba, Hispaniola, Puerto Rico, and Jamaica. There were probably about one million Taíno living in Hispaniola when Columbus arrived in 1492.

Historians believe that the Taíno first came to the Caribbean around 1000 B.C. They were primarily farmers, but also fished and hunted for food. Columbus and his crew were the first Europeans to meet the Taíno. Columbus, thinking he was in India, mistakenly called the Taíno "Indians."

Although today some people claim to be descended from the Taíno, most historians believe that Taíno society was destroyed during the 1700s. The natives had no resistance to diseases brought by European settlers, and many died. Others became slaves or married Spanish settlers or African slaves.[26]

On October 11, the sailors saw flowers and branches in the water. At 2:00 the next morning, a lookout saw a stretch of sand shining in the moonlight. The long journey was finally over. Thirty-three days after leaving the Canary Islands, Columbus had reached his goal—or so he thought. Because his calculations about the size of the Ocean Sea and the amount of land that covered the earth were incorrect, it made perfect sense to him that he had reached Asia after sailing for thirty-three days.

Columbus and his men landed early in the morning of October 12, 1492. He claimed the land for Spain. Meanwhile, groups of native people came to stare at these curious visitors. Because he thought he was in the Indies, Columbus called these people Indians. Columbus did not realize it yet, but he was not in the Indies at all. Instead, he had landed on an island no one in Europe even knew about.

Columbus explored these new lands. He named his landing place San Salvador, which means "Holy Savior." This island is still known as San Salvador today, although many historians have suggested other landing places on the many islands around the Bahamas and Cuba.[27]

When Columbus and his men reached land, Columbus claimed it for Spain.

Later, Columbus visited another island and named it La Isla Espanola, or "the Spanish Isle." This island later became known as Hispaniola and is still called that today.

Columbus thought these lands were very beautiful, but he did not find any gold or riches there. Then his biggest ship, the *Santa Maria*, was damaged when it ran aground on a coral reef. Finally, on January 4, 1493, Columbus and most of his men set sail back to Spain. They took seven of the island people with them. Columbus wrote that he "caused [them] to be taken in order to carry them away to [Your Highnesses] and to learn our language and to return them."[28]

Christopher Columbus arrived in Palos, Spain, on March 14, 1493. He rested there for ten days, waiting to hear from King Ferdinand and Queen Isabella. When he received an invitation to come to court, Columbus's party included the island people he had brought to Spain. He also brought many exotic gifts, including parrots and jeweled masks and belts.

Columbus arrived in Barcelona, Spain, in mid-April. The streets near the harbor were jammed with people, all eager to see Columbus, the island people, and the many treasures he brought back.[29] Columbus was hailed as a national hero. The king and queen named him the "Admiral of the Ocean Sea." His discovery was exciting news. Everyone wondered what riches these new lands held. Columbus was determined to find out.

Columbus made three more voyages to the New World between 1493 and 1502. During these voyages, he founded a permanent Spanish colony on Hispaniola. He named the colony Isabela after

Hispaniola

Hispaniola is the second largest Caribbean island. Cuba is the largest. The indigenous Taíno people called Hispaniola Quisqueya.

While the Spanish settled the eastern part of the island, the French settled the west. In 1697, Spain recognized French control of the western third of the island. Later, this part of the island became the nation of Haiti. The eastern part of the island became known as the Dominican Republic. Although there were wars between Haiti and the Dominican Republic during the 1790s and again in 1821–1822, the two nations exist peacefully today.

the queen. Columbus also made a list of about seven hundred islands he "discovered."

Columbus's arrival brought devastating changes to the people who lived on the islands. Many were killed in battles with the European settlers. Many more died of diseases introduced by the new settlers. Columbus was also responsible for introducing the horrors of slavery to the New World. In February 1494, Columbus sent a letter to Spain with Antonio de Torres, the captain of a returning ship. Although Queen Isabella was very much against slavery, Columbus suggested that some Caribbean people should be captured and sent into slavery because they were cannibals:

> For the good of the souls of the said cannibals . . . the thought has occurred to us that the greater the number that are sent over to Spain the better. . . . [The Caribees] are a wild people, fit for any work, well proportioned and very intelligent, and who, when they have got rid of the cruel habits to which they have become accustomed, will be better than any other kind of slaves.[30]

Queen Isabella said no, but Columbus went on with his plan anyway. He also made the island people mine gold for the Spanish invaders under a brutal system of forced labor.[31]

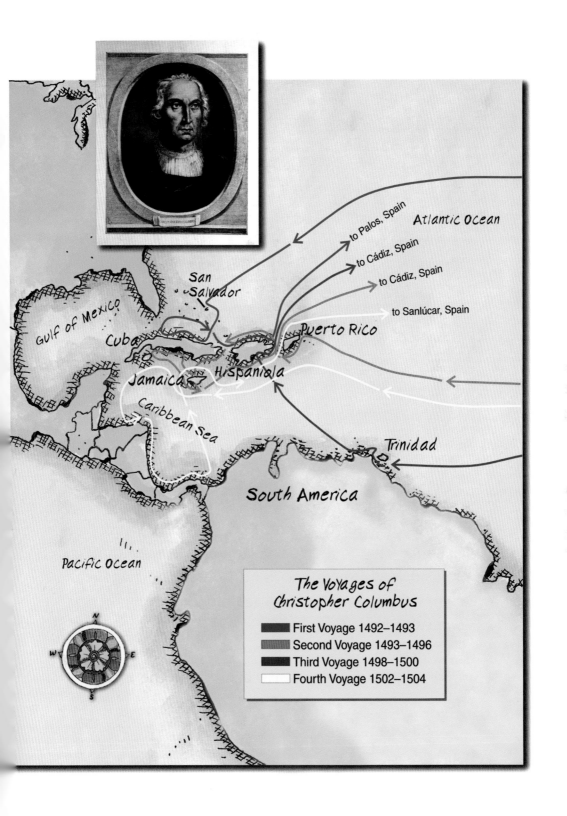

to Palos, Spain

Atlantic Ocean

to Cádiz, Spain

to Cádiz, Spain

to Sanlúcar, Spain

San Salvador

Gulf of Mexico

Cuba

Puerto Rico

Hispaniola

Jamaica

Caribbean Sea

Trinidad

South America

Pacific Ocean

The Voyages of Christopher Columbus

First Voyage 1492–1493
Second Voyage 1493–1496
Third Voyage 1498–1500
Fourth Voyage 1502–1504

Columbus was a brilliant navigator, but he was a poor administrator who did not get along well with others. His poor management left the colony of Isabela in such bad shape that in 1500, Spain sent Francisco de Bobadilla to rule in Columbus's place. Bobadilla sent Columbus back to Spain in chains. Although the king and queen restored his freedom and even allowed Columbus to make one more voyage in 1502, he was also stripped of many of his titles. In addition, Columbus lost the respect of most of the Spanish people.[32]

Columbus died in Spain on May 20, 1506. Although his voyages had made him rich, at the time of his death he was almost forgotten because Spain had hired other explorers to continue the exploration and settlement of what began to be called the New World. Centuries passed before his name became famous again.

In an odd twist of fate, the new lands Columbus had sailed to were not even named after him. Instead, North and South America got their names from an Italian navigator and mapmaker named Amerigo Vespucci.

Amerigo Vespucci

Amerigo Vespucci, an Italian explorer and writer, was born in Florence, Italy, in 1454. In 1499, Vespucci joined a Spanish expedition to the West Indies. After landing in what is now Guyana, Vespucci left the rest of the group. He continued sailing south until he reached the mouth of the Amazon River, then returned to Spain in 1500. Vespucci sailed again in 1501–1502 and reached what is now Rio de Janeiro.

Vespucci wrote about his travels and announced he had discovered a new continent. In 1507, a German named Martin Waldseemüller created a world map and called the new continent America after the Latin form of Vespucci's first name, Americus.[33]

However, historians are not sure if Vespucci told the truth. They point to claims that he made about a 1497 voyage to the New World—a voyage which definitely did not take place. Vespucci also said he sailed far south along the coast of South America, but since he did not describe notable landmarks, he may have exaggerated that too. Other historians think that Vespucci did not write his famous letters at all, but that the documents were forged by another explorer.

Christopher Columbus

3

The History of Columbus Day

During the years of the American Revolution, many Americans began to look for ways to establish a strong national identity. This effort included a close look at the beginnings of settlements in the New World. Columbus's voyages were rediscovered, and people began to look for ways to honor him. Many felt that the explorer symbolized the idea of America "as a new land of opportunity, possibility, and progress."[1] The idea spread through newspapers, letters, and public speeches. During the 1760s, Columbus began to appear in songs and poems celebrating liberty and calling for independence from Great Britain.[2] It helped that Columbus was not British. One historian noted that Columbus gave America "a past that bypassed England."[3] By the 1770s, the American colonies were frequently called Columba or Columbia in honor of the explorer. Columbia also became the female symbol of the United States, just as Uncle Sam became the male symbol of the nation. This female figure often represented the United States in political cartoons, usually dressed in a flowing gown and holding the American flag.[4]

George Washington

Columbus's name soon became linked with another hero, George Washington. Washington was often called "the father of his country." He received this honor because his leadership, both as an army commander in the American Revolution and later as the nation's first president, was vitally important in establishing the new nation. Washington was a contemporary figure, while Columbus was a European from the past.

George Washington

George Washington was born on February 22, 1732. He grew up on a wealthy plantation in Virginia, which was then a British colony. Later, Washington became a surveyor and traveled throughout much of the Virginia colony.

Washington first became famous when he served as an officer during the French and Indian War. Later, he led a local militia supporting the British Empire in America. However, Washington's feelings about British rule changed, and he soon became allied with colonists fighting for independence. When the American Revolution started in 1775, Washington was named Commander in Chief of the American army. He held this post until the war ended with an American victory in 1783. In 1787, he led the Constitutional Convention, which drafted the current United States Constitution.

Washington was such a good leader and was so popular that he was the unanimous choice to be the first president of the United States. He set many policies that are still in place today.

Washington chose to leave the presidency in 1797, after serving two terms. George Washington died December 14, 1799.

"The combination of references to the new and old worlds gave stability to the nation's identity."[5]

In 1789, Washington decided that a site between Virginia and Maryland would be the new capital of the United States, and both states were asked to give up some land to create the new city. To honor both Washington and Columbus, commissioners from Virginia and Maryland decided to name the area after both heroes. In a September 9, 1791, letter to Pierre L'Enfant, the city's designer, the commissioners wrote:

> We have agreed that the federal district shall be called 'The Territory of Columbia,' and the Federal City, 'The City of Washington': the title of the map, will, therefore, be 'A Map of the City of Washington, in the Territory of Columbia.'[6]

Later, the city became known as Washington, District of Columbia, or Washington, D.C.

Although Columbus was honored by the name of the United States capital, it was New York City that shaped Columbus Day as a national celebration. In 1789, a group called the Society of St. Tammany, or the Columbian Order, was founded in New York City. The society's motto was "Freedom Our Rock," and its goal was to connect patriotism to political rights and freedoms. The society was

The Capitol building in Washington, D.C., is named for George Washington and Christopher Columbus.

named after two figures. Tammany, also known as Tamanend, was a 17th-century chief of the Lenni Lenape, an American Indian tribe that lived in what later became Pennsylvania. Tammany signed a peace treaty with William Penn, the founder of Pennsylvania, in 1683 and was known for the motto "Unite in peace for happiness; in war for defense."[7]

Tammany represented the New World (America), while Columbus represented the Old World (Europe).[8] The Society of St. Tammany specified that October 12 would be the day to honor Columbus and his arrival in America. In 1790 and 1791, this date was marked with a dinner and many speeches and tributes to Columbus.

William Penn signed a treaty for peace.

The 300th anniversary of Columbus's arrival in the New World occurred in 1792 and the Society of St. Tammany decided to mark the event in style. The society held a dinner and official ceremony to commemorate the event. The order also dedicated a 15-foot-tall monument to Columbus in New York City.[9] The monument was placed in the American Museum of the Tammany Society, which was located in lower Manhattan. Later, it was exhibited at other museums and eventually became part of the collection of the great showman P. T. Barnum. Unfortunately, the monument disappeared, and no trace of it remains today.

P. T. Barnum

Born in 1810 in Connecticut, Phineas Taylor Barnum began his career as a showman in 1835. He set up an exhibit showing Joice Heth, an aged slave who claimed to have been George Washington's nurse. In 1841, Barnum became owner of the American Museum in New York City. It was one of the city's most famous attractions. It burned down in 1865, was reopened, then burned down again in 1868.

Barnum became Charles Sherwood Stratton's manager in 1842. Stratton was renamed General Tom Thumb. They toured Europe and Barnum made a fortune. Barnum also took singer Jenny Lind under his wing and managed her United States concert tour.

Perhaps most people know Barnum's name from the circus. Known today as the Ringling Brothers and Barnum & Bailey Circus, Barnum opened his "Greatest Show on Earth" in 1871.

The Society of St. Tammany's celebrations were written up in many newspapers. These stories inspired other cities to hold their own Columbus Day celebrations. Boston, Massachusetts; Providence, Rhode Island; Richmond, Virginia; and several smaller cities and towns held parades, dinners, and toasts to honor the occasion.[10]

During the 1800s, many immigrants began coming to the United States in search of more opportunities and a better life. Some of these immigrants were Italian. As they became part of American society, Italian social groups began to focus on Columbus's fame. These groups saw him as a shining example of Italian achievement and wanted to share their pride with the nation. Italians in New York City organized a celebration on October 12, 1866. The holiday received its official name in 1869, when Italians in San Francisco called October 12 "Columbus Day" for the first time.[11]

During the nation's centennial celebration in 1876, Italians in Philadelphia, Pennsylvania, raised money to build a statue of Columbus in the city's Fairmount Park. By 1877, Italian organizations in many American cities were honoring Columbus with parades, speeches, banquets, and dances. Christopher Columbus was increasingly identified with immigrants, and his presence allowed new Americans to "declare their long-standing American identity, asserting and laying claim to their rightful place in Columbia."[12]

America's Catholics, who were largely immigrants of Irish, Italian, and Hispanic origin, also found a role model and hero in Columbus, a

Catholic explorer. In 1882, a group of Irish-Catholic men in New Haven, Connecticut, worked with their parish priest to found a Catholic men's organization called the Knights of Columbus. These men felt they were treated as second-class citizens because of their Catholic faith. As one man explained, they chose the name Knights of Columbus to show "we Catholics were no aliens to this country, but were entitled to all rights and privileges due to such Discovery by one of our faith."[13]

In 1892, the federal government decided on a national celebration for the 400th anniversary of Christopher Columbus's discovery. The celebration would be a huge fair located in Chicago, Illinois. However, despite federal funding, it was not possible for the government to complete the buildings needed to house the exhibits in time for a celebration in 1892. Instead, the Columbian Exposition was held in Chicago between May and October of 1893. Millions of people came from all over the world to see the exposition, which included replicas of Columbus's three ships and a large statue of Columbus himself. Congress also asked President Grover Cleveland to issue a proclamation urging all Americans to observe the anniversary "by suitable exercises in their school and other places of assembly."[14] These exercises

Some people have recreated Columbus's three ships.

included speeches, costumed presentations, and patriotic songs. Columbus Day was also celebrated in other American cities. New York City held a five-day extravaganza that included parades, fireworks, and other public demonstrations.

Over the next few years, many states began to honor Christopher Columbus. In 1905, Colorado became the first state to observe Columbus Day as an official holiday. By 1910, Columbus Day was an annual holiday in fifteen states, and thirty-four states celebrated the day by 1938. That year, President Franklin Roosevelt proclaimed every October 12 as Columbus Day. Finally, in 1971, the holiday was changed to the second

Grover Cleveland

Monday in October, as were several other holidays, in order to create a number of three-day weekends in the calendar. At this time, Columbus Day also became a federal and state holiday.[15] Today, Columbus Day is a day to think about a brave Italian explorer and honor his heritage and accomplishments.

CHRISTOPHER·COLVMBVS

The Cultural Significance of Columbus Day

Columbus Day has great cultural significance to many Americans. It is a day to honor an important man in American history. It is also a day when Italian Americans pay tribute to their heritage.

Italian Americans have taken Columbus to heart for more than two hundred years. As waves of Italian immigrants came to the United States during the late 1800s and early 1900s, they faced tremendous discrimination. Many Italian-American organizations, such as the Sons of Italy, were formed to provide their members with a sense of community. These organizations helped immigrants succeed in America and overcome the prejudice and discrimination they faced.

Italian Americans chose Columbus as a hero who instilled pride in the ethnic community. By claiming an American hero as one of their own, Italians were able to show pride in themselves and also in their adopted homeland of America.

Italian Americans also liked the image of Columbus as an immigrant. Like Columbus, Italian immigrants had left behind everything they knew to search for a new land. They had "made their own voyages of discovery . . . and built a new world in America for themselves and their children."[1]

Columbus Day is also a patriotic holiday. This is especially true in schools throughout the United States. Columbus became part of American school lessons during the earliest days of the nation. Books such as *Geography Made Easy*, published in 1784 by Jedidiah Morse, included a lengthy essay about Columbus's life and his voyages. Noah Webster's 1787 collection, *An American Selection of Lessons in Reading and Speaking*, also featured an extensive biography of Columbus.[2]

History books began to appear in schools around 1820. These books featured Columbus as the beginning of the nation's history. He was also used to demonstrate the virtues young Americans should have, such as bravery, confidence, patience, and enterprise.[3]

By the time of the 400th anniversary of Columbus's voyages, American schoolchildren were important parts of Columbus Day celebrations. In June 1892, President Benjamin Harrison declared that October 12, 1892, would be a general holiday to celebrate Columbus's achievements. He called for schools to be the center of the celebration. A national magazine called *The Youth's Companion* published a program of events for the day, and urged all children who subscribed to share it with their teachers so that no child or school would be left out. The program called for schoolchildren to assemble around the flagpole at 9:00 A.M. and be joined by a group of Civil War veterans. They would read a proclamation from the president, raise the flag, give a military salute, recite the

Benjamin Harrison

In schools throughout the United States children make crafts and learn about Christopher Columbus.

Pledge of Allegiance, and sing "My Country 'tis of Thee." The program would continue with an original Columbus Day song and several speeches.[4]

Schools participated in Columbus Day celebrations in other ways in 1892. In New York

City, about twelve thousand public schoolchildren and fifty-five hundred Catholic schoolchildren took part in the city's parade to honor Columbus. Schoolchildren in other cities also marched in local parades.

Today, schoolchildren learn about Columbus from a very early age. They recite poems such as the famous, "In fourteen hundred and ninety-two, Columbus sailed the ocean blue,"[5] and create arts and crafts projects based on Columbus's voyages. These projects include making boats out of walnut shells or egg cartons, drawing pictures and making models of Columbus's three ships, or creating maps to show Columbus's voyages to the New World. Children continue to march in Columbus Day parades, representing both their schools and civic organizations such as the Girl Scouts and Boy Scouts. This participation continues a patriotic tradition that has been alive since the founding of the United States.

Columbus Day is also a day of cultural significance for Hispanic Americans and American Indians, although it is not usually seen in a positive way. For many members of these ethnic groups, Christopher Columbus is a symbol of the European destruction of the native way of life that existed in the Americas for millennia before

Spanish Influence in the Americas

The Spanish settlers changed life in the Americas in many ways. Their effect on the native people was devastating. America's indigenous peoples were forced into slavery. Thousands died of diseases brought to the New World by the Spanish. Entire cultures were wiped out as the Spanish imposed their values, ways of life, and religion on the native tribes.

Native cultures were also weakened when they intermarried with the Spanish. This was especially true in Mexico, where the descendents of native people and Spaniards formed a class known as *mestizos*. Mestizos were not given the same rights as full-blooded Spanish.

Spanish culture, language, and religion destroyed most aspects of the native cultures Columbus and other explorers found in the Americas.[6]

1492. Columbus is seen as beginning the wave of European exploration and colonization that led to the deaths of millions of native people and the enslavement of millions more.

The arrival of Spaniards changed every part of American Indian life. Not only was the native culture destroyed, but its religious beliefs were forever altered as well. Roman Catholicism was the official religion of Spain, and Spain was eager to spread this religion among the natives of the New World. Spanish officials and missionaries were so successful in spreading the Roman Catholic religion in the New World and converting its inhabitants to the faith that, today, one third of the people in Latin America are Catholic.[7] In the words of one Catholic priest in Mexico, "There is not a real Latin American Church. We have a Spanish Church, changed a little bit, imported. [The Spanish] brought the whole package, and said, everything you have is wrong, here is salvation and life for you."[8]

The negative feelings of American Indians for Columbus Day were especially evident in 1992, the 500th anniversary of the explorer's first visit to the New World. Many holiday celebrations were interrupted by American Indian protesters. Stephanie Betancourt, the Seneca tribal coordinator of the Native American Education Program, expressed the protesters' feelings when she said, "For Native Americans, every Columbus Day is like salt in our wounds. These are days of mourning."[9]

However, some Hispanics express a different opinion. They feel that Columbus Day is the "cultural birthday" of Hispanics because Columbus sailed under the Spanish flag. As one writer put it,

Protestors of Columbus Day spray painted this statue of Christopher Columbus in Washington, D.C.

Some Hispanics—here in the United States as well as in Latin America—proudly consider Columbus Day a cultural birthday, the beginning of a historical process that made the Hispanic world what it is today. . . . Without Columbus, without the conquistadors that followed him, without colonization by Spain and Portugal, a Latin America would not exist.[10]

Indeed, many of today's Hispanics are the descendants of both the native people and the Spanish settlers who conquered them. They are all part of what is called *la raza*, or "the race." La raza is a combination of many different cultures, which can give mixed feelings to Hispanics who want to take pride in all of their ancestors.

The view that the Spanish conquistadors are an important part of Hispanic Americans' cultural identity does not mean that the cruelty of the Spanish conquerors was justified. It also does not deny the fact that entire cultures were destroyed by the Europeans. However, this view does make it clear that the Latin America we know today was shaped by Columbus's voyage. All of American history was shaped by that journey too.

People show their pride during a Columbus Day parade in New York City.

Who Celebrates Columbus Day?

Columbus Day is a day all Americans can celebrate. However, although many take part in community celebrations, most Americans see the day as little more than a holiday from work or school.

Most large Columbus Day celebrations are held in major cities. Cities such as New York hold large parades. Marchers in these parades include members of Italian-American and Catholic organizations, as well as school marching bands, troops of Boy Scouts and Girl Scouts, and members of the police and fire departments. The grand marshal, or leader, of the parade is usually a well-respected Italian American who is known in the community for his or her work in charitable, political, or business organizations.

Some cities have extended Columbus Day into a series of festivals. Since 1995, San Diego's Little Italy neighborhood has been host to a Columbus Day Festa. The colorful festival features Italian music and dancing, such as a lively dance called the tarantella, along with street painting and a variety of food and craft booths highlighting the best in Italian cuisine and artifacts. Traditional Italian foods, such as calzones, pasta, and rich, custard-filled pastries called cannoli, are among the Italian foods available at this festival.[1]

Columbus Day is a federal holiday. That means government offices, banks, and schools are closed. Some businesses close as well, but many others remain open. For many Americans, the holiday provides a three-day weekend and a chance for people to enjoy themselves. However, most Americans spend the day doing activities that have nothing to do with Christopher Columbus. Many Americans take vacations over the long weekend. Others shop, visit friends, attend sporting events, or simply relax at home. Merchants advertise

These women and girls wear traditional
Italian dresses for the 2005 Columbus Day
parade in New York City.

Columbus Day sales, using the holiday as an excuse to get customers into their stores. Although every American knows who Columbus was, many have forgotten the meaning of the day.

Día de la Raza

In Latin America, Columbus Day is a time to focus more on Hispanic culture than on the explorer himself. In Latin America, as well as in some Latino communities in the United States, the holiday is known as Día de la Raza, or "Day of the Race." This holiday commemorates the first meetings between Europeans and Native Americans and the Hispanic culture, race, and identity that arose from the mixture of two very different cultures.[2] Día de la Raza was first celebrated in Argentina in 1917. Venezuela began celebrating this holiday in 1921, Chile in 1923, and Mexico in 1928.[3]

Jose Limon, director of the Center for Mexican American Studies in Texas, explains the origins of Día de la Raza: "Columbus Day acknowledges just the Spanish discovery of America," he says. "That was a problematic thing for people in Latin America."[4] The Latin American community felt a day was needed to "celebrate the indigenous people and the culture that developed when they incorporated European influences" without forgetting the

These women parade through a street in Mexico City, Mexico, during Día de la Raza. In the background, a statue of Christopher Columbus is covered to protect it from protesters. It was not harmed during the parade.

"misery that the Spaniards brought during the next three hundred years of their colonial rule."[5]

Día de la Raza tries to make people aware of the indigenous cultures that were present in America before Columbus arrived. Events educate people about indigenous culture, celebrate native history, and show how native traditions have remained alive today through art, music, dance, and poetry.[6]

Street performers in traditional American Indian dress perform during a Columbus Day celebration in Mexico City, Mexico.

Symbols of Columbus Day

Symbols of Columbus Day include pictures of Columbus, Queen Isabella and King Ferdinand of Spain, and Columbus's three ships, the *Niña*, the *Pinta*, and the *Santa María*. These images are the focus of many Columbus Day–themed school projects. Children draw and color pictures of the explorer and Spain's king and queen. They also read about, draw, and make models of Columbus's three ships.

Some schools put on plays about Columbus and his voyage. These plays re-enact the explorer's struggle to find support for his voyage, his long journey across the sea, and his first meetings with American Indians.

Columbus's journeys have a celebration in Columbus, Ohio. This city is the largest community named after the explorer. In 1992, a replica of Columbus's flagship, the *Santa María*, was placed in the Scioto River in the city's center. The boat is open for tours and special events and is visited by schoolchildren and other groups. The *Santa María* is run by a private foundation with financial support from the city. The foundation's goals are to commemorate and interpret Columbus's voyage, as well as the sailing traditions and culture and life of its crew; to serve as an educational museum to teach the importance and impact of Columbus's voyage, as well as the technology of the day; and to

Niña　　　　Pinta　　　　Santa María

Replicas of the *Niña*, *Pinta*, and *Santa María* sail the seas.

As a gift from Palermo, a city on the Italian island of Sicily, this float was in the 2003 New York City Columbus Day parade.

A replica of the *Niña* sets sail for Indiana.

represent the city of Columbus and encourage people to visit the city and surrounding area.[1]

Many cities hold Columbus Day parades. These parades include many symbols of the day. These symbols include floats showing

Queen Isabella, King Ferdinand, and, of course, Columbus. Other floats show Columbus's three ships. Some marchers wear costumes modeled on 15th-century clothes to show how Columbus and his men dressed. These costumes include long, colorful robes made of rich fabrics such as velvet and brocade. Men's fashions of the day included short, wide shirts, called doublets, with high, stiff collars. Doublets were worn over thick stockings called hose. Men also wore short, full pants, called breeches, that were often padded to make them appear even wider. Nobles and other wealthy men also wore extravagantly decorated hats in a variety of shapes and styles.[2] Traditional fashions such as these, along with other symbols of Columbus's era, help people remember his voyages and the times he lived in.

Columbus Day Today

Columbus Day is celebrated every year in the United States. Most public celebrations of Columbus Day are held in major cities with a large Italian population. New York City holds the largest Columbus Day parade in the United States, complete with floats, marching bands, Italian-American civic groups, and Italian-American politicians.

Although Columbus is still viewed as an important figure in American history and Columbus Day is still a major holiday, the explorer and his holiday have come under fire in recent years. Historians point out that Columbus was not even the first European to arrive in the New World. Credit for that is generally given to the Vikings because archaeological evidence shows that they arrived in L'Anse aux Meadows in Newfoundland, Canada, and set up short-lived settlements there as far back as the early 1000s, almost five hundred years before Columbus arrived. Columbus also never set foot on the United States mainland. Instead, he landed on an island in the Bahamas, which is not part of the United States.[1]

Although Columbus was previously called the "discoverer" of America, American Indian groups pointed out that they had been living in America for centuries before Columbus "discovered" it. Calling a European the discoverer of America was an insult to their native culture. It also ignored the fact that the arrival of the Europeans signaled the end of the native way of life.

In the past, the feelings of Americans Indians were not respected or even considered. Most of the many celebrations held in 1892 for the 400th anniversary of Columbus's voyage barely mentioned American Indians. When they did, the most common view was that the natives had benefited

The Vikings

Many historians believe that the Spanish were not the first Europeans to set foot in America. Some give that distinction to the Viking culture that flourished more than one thousand years ago.

The Vikings were warriors who lived in Scandinavia, the far northern part of Europe. Between the eighth and eleventh centuries, Viking warriors were feared throughout Scandinavia, Great Britain, Russia, and other parts of Europe because of their daring raids. These raids left villages burned, inhabitants murdered, and treasures stolen. The Vikings were such an important force that the period between A.D. 793 and 1006 is often called the Viking Age.

The Vikings were fearless travelers, and several ventured far beyond Europe. Perhaps the most famous Viking explorer was Leif

(continued on next page)

A statue of Leif Eriksson

The Vikings *(continued from previous page)*

Eriksson. He was born in Iceland around 975, but later moved to Greenland when his father, Erik the Red, was exiled for murder. In 1001, Eriksson left Greenland to explore lands to the west. Within a few weeks, he and his crew landed in a heavily wooded land. Eriksson named the place "Markland." Today, historians believe it is part of Labrador, in eastern Canada. Later, Eriksson traveled south. He and his men spent the winter in a place he named Vinland, because of the grape vines that grew there. Vinland was probably L'Anse aux Meadows in Newfoundland, Canada. Eriksson and his men very well might have been the first European visitors to the New World.

Eriksson returned to Greenland, where he died in 1020. Other Vikings traveled to the land that is now Canada. The Viking Age soon ended and so did that culture's exploration of the New World. However, Viking culture and history live on, along with the mystery of how far west they actually traveled.

from being "discovered."[2] Educator Thomas Morgan, for example, wrote that Columbus and his followers had destroyed native civilization, while at the same time he encouraged "the complete integration of the natives into white American culture, where they could become part of a richer, broader mainstream."[3] Even those who acknowledged that Europeans had destroyed native civilizations celebrated Columbus's accomplishments as an explorer.

Public opinion had changed radically by the time the United States began preparing for the 500th anniversary in 1992. During the 1950s and 1960s, Americans had become increasingly aware that the many different ethnic groups and cultures in the United States deserved respect and equal treatment, and that the accepted history of America did not always represent these groups fairly. These decades saw the flourishing of the civil rights movement, which featured people of all races marching and demonstrating to ensure that all people were treated fairly, no matter the color of their skin or where their ancestors had come from.

Many ethnic groups saw the 500th anniversary as a time to speak out against Columbus's legacy and make the rest of America more aware of the truth. In a 1989 interview, Rayna Green, director of the American Indian Program for the Smithsonian National Museum of Natural History, said,

> This is an extraordinary opportunity to talk about the invasion of North America and the

things we are still living with. . . . We've got to take this occasion to talk about what is affecting our people even today.[4]

American Indian groups even interrupted several major parades and protested at other celebrations to make their feelings clear.

Columbus was suddenly looked at in a whole different light. Instead of a bearer of civilization, he was transformed into the source of contemporary evil.[5] Many people agreed that Columbus was not a man to be celebrated. In an article in the *New York Amsterdam News*, William Loren Katz, a historian and professor at New York University who has published more than forty books, asked, "Must we celebrate another Columbus Day? . . . Columbus was merely the first conqueror of a 'New World' ruled by Native Americans for 3,000 years. He introduced slavery, exploitation, and death to the most populated part of the globe, 18 million in North America alone. . . . What we need is a holiday to celebrate the upwards of 75,000,000 people who lived here in peace in 1492 and then mounted a resistance."[6] (Katz's numbers include the native populations of North and South America.) Katz went on to state that "Columbus's goals were not the kind taught in schools. He sought the victory of Christianity

These protesters are a part of a community-based organization that is against Columbus Day.

throughout the universe. . . . Gold consumed his thoughts: In his diary, in the first two weeks in the Americas, he mentions gold 75 times."[7]

Another outspoken opponent of Columbus Day is Ward Churchill, a controversial professor of ethnic studies at the University of Colorado at Boulder and a leader of the American Indian Movement of Colorado. Churchill has argued that Columbus Day "contributes to the perpetuation of genocidal policies against Indians" and makes it clear that such cruelty is "neither acceptable or unimportant." He goes on to say that "Undeniably, the situation American Indians will not—in fact *cannot*—change for the better so long as such attitudes are deemed socially acceptable . . . such celebrations as Columbus Day *must* be stopped."[8]

Many Italian Americans, however, were reluctant to give up their hero. When protesters blocked a downtown parade in Denver, Colorado, chanting "No parades for murderers," the president of the Italian-American Organization of Denver insisted that the city's Columbus Day celebrations were meant to honor all people, and that Columbus was a bridge between two worlds.[9] Similarly, Governor Mario Cuomo of New York, who is of Italian descent, said the day celebrated more

Protesters blocked a Columbus Day parade
in Denver, Colorado.

than just the man. "Christopher Columbus pushed open the door to 500 years of progress," he stated. "What we're celebrating today is 500 years of the American experience."[10]

With the approaching 500th anniversary, various ethnic groups tried to work together to re-create the holiday as a celebration of ethnic diversity and accomplishment. The Reverend Chris Iosso, a Presbyterian minister, wrote,

> My worry is that in reassigning the good-guy/ bad-guy roles in the past, we limit and polarize the roles given to racial and ethnic groups in the current context. While it is certainly part of the point that European-Americans have never stopped oppressing Native peoples at some level, that Euro-presence is also responsible for quite a number of other developments, good and bad. . . . As Americans, we need bigger symbols than Columbus or St. Patrick and the Pilgrims, and as Christians it is partly our job to help develop or renew inclusive symbols.[11]

Iosso's point is that no ethnic group or culture is entirely good or entirely bad. People must not limit their views by focusing on symbols that only tell one side of the story. History is too complex for such a simple view.

In an effort to change the perspective of the holiday, many groups have suggested changing the name and the focus of the celebrations. In 1989, South Dakota, which has a large American Indian population, renamed the holiday Native American Day.[12] In 1992, the Presbyterian Synod of the Northeast also voted to rename Columbus Day as Native American Day.[13] Some have encouraged the celebration of "Indigenous Peoples Day" or "Ethnic Diversity Day" to honor American Indians and Hispanic Americans. Others have suggested combining Columbus Day celebrations with the Latin American holiday Día de la Raza.

Our views of Columbus have changed drastically since the first celebration in 1792. However, there is no denying that he is an important figure in American history, a man who forever changed the color and history of America's people. As religious historian Gerald P. Fogarty has written, "Somewhere between the icon and the idol remains the truth. The task of the historian . . . is to search for that truth and gain some objectivity."[14] Although the focus of the day has changed, Columbus Day will remain an important national holiday in the United States for many years to come.

Find Your Way!

Christopher Columbus did not have the modern conveniences we have today to help him sail the seas. Pretend you are an explorer, and use only a compass, paper, and a pencil to map out your route to school, your house, the mall, park, or other favorite place. Be sure to ask an adult for permission and help.

What you will need:

✓ **compass**

✓ **pad of paper**

✓ **pencil**

1. Decide on the route you are going to map out. Are you going from home to school? From school to home? On the pad of paper, write down from where you are starting.

2. Count your steps as you walk to your favorite place. If an adult is driving, ask how many miles you have gone. Write down the number of steps you have walked, or how many miles you have gone. Keep track of any turns and write them down. Do you pass any landmarks? Any big trees? Big buildings? Statues? Write down anything that will help you remember your way.

3 Look at your compass. What direction does it say you are going? Write that down.

4 When you get to your final location, look at everything you have written down about your journey. Do you think you could return to the starting location by following the directions in reverse? Try it!

5 Imagine what Christopher Columbus went through to sail the seas!

GLOSSARY

arrogant—Conceited or too proud.

calculated—Figured out.

calzone—Pizza dough folded in half filled with various toppings, most often including cheese.

cannibals—People who eat other people.

cannoli—An Italian pastry filled with custard or sweetened ricotta cheese.

city-states—A type of government made up of a city and the surrounding area.

commemorates—Does something special to honor a person or event.

commissioners—People empowered to work together to solve a problem or complete a task.

conquistadors—Spanish conquerors of the New World.

controversial—Something that causes an argument.

federal—Having to do with a nation formed by combining several states or nations.

flagship—The most important ship in a fleet.

genocidal—Having to do with the deliberate destruction of a group of people.

infidels—People who do not believe in a particular religion.

mainland—The chief landmass of a country or continent.

missionaries—People sent by a church to teach that group's faith to others.

navigate—To travel using maps, the stars, instruments, or calculations for guidance.

replicas—Exact copies.

tarantella—A fast Italian folk dance.

trade winds—Winds that blow in a northeasterly direction across the Atlantic Ocean.

treasury—Money controlled by a government.

tributes—Speeches or demonstrations that show thanks or respect for a person.

CHAPTER NOTES

◈ Chapter 1. Land!

1. John Noble Wilford, *The Mysterious History of Columbus: An Exploration of the Man, the Myth, the Legacy* (New York: Alfred A. Knopf, 1991), p. 129.
2. Ibid., p. 129.
3. Ibid., p. 147.
4. Ibid., p. 159.

◈ Chapter 2. The Life of Christopher Columbus

1. J. H. Elliott, *The Old World and the New, 1492–1650* (Cambridge, England: Cambridge University Press, 1992, p. 10.
2. Samuel Eliot Morison, *Admiral of the Ocean Sea: A Life of Christopher Columbus* (Boston: Little, Brown and Company, 1942), pp. 15–16.
3. "Indies," Wikipedia, n.d., <http://en.wikipedia.org/wiki/Indies> (February 27, 2006).
4. Zvi Dor-Ner, *Columbus and the Age of Discovery* (New York: William Morrow and Company, 1991), p. 29.
5. Ibid., p. 40.
6. Patty Strassman, "The Influence of Spice Trade on the Age of Discovery," n.d., <http://muweb.millersville.edu/~columbus/papers/strass-1.html>
7. Claudia L. Bushman, *America Discovers Columbus: How an Italian Explorer Became an American Hero* (Hanover, N. H.: University Press of New England, 1992), p. 15.
8. Dor-Ner, p. 34.

9. Morison, p. 22.
10. "Marco Polo," Wikipedia, n.d.,<http://en.wikipedia. org/wiki/Marco_Polo> (February 27, 2006).
11. John Noble, Wilford, *The Mysterious History of Columbus: An Exploration of the Man, the Myth, the Legacy* (New York: Alfred A. Knopf, 1991), p. 80.
12. Dor-Ner, p. 86.
13. Ibid., p. 87.
14. Ibid.
15. Ibid., p. 101.
16. "Ferdinand V," and "Isabella I," Microsoft Encarta 2000 CD-ROM.
17. "Catholic Monarchs," Wikipedia, n.d., <http://en. wikipedia.org/wiki/Catholic_Monarch> (February 27, 2006).
18. Ferdinand Columbus, *The Life of the Admiral Christopher Columbus by His Son Ferdinand*, translated and annotated by Benjamin Keen (New Brunswick, N.J.: Rutgers University Press, 1959), p. 43.
19. Dor-Ner, pp. 131–132.
20. Ibid., p. 135.
21. Ibid., pp. 125–126.
22. Ibid., p. 139.
23. Ibid., p. 142.
24. Oliver Dunn and James E. Kelley, *The Diario of Christopher Columbus's First Voyage to America, 1492–1493* (Norman: University of Oklahoma Press, 1989), p. 29.
25. Dor-Ner, p. 144.
26. "Taino," Wikipedia, n.d., <http://en.wikipedia.org/ wiki/Taino> (February 27, 2006).
27. Wilford, p. 133.
28. Ibid., p. 150.
29. Ibid., p. 24.

30. R. H. Major, trans., *Christopher Columbus: Four Voyages to the New World; Letters and Selected Documents* (New York: Corinth Books, 1961), pp. 84–85.

31. Dor-Ner, p. 215.

32. Wilford, p. 204.

33. "Amerigo Vespucci," Wikipedia, n.d. <http://en.wiki pedia.org/wiki/Amerigo_Vespucci> (February 27, 2006).

◈ Chapter 3. **The History of Columbus Day**

1. Matthew Dennis, *Red, White, and Blue Letter Days: An American Calendar* (Ithaca, N.Y.: Cornell University Press, 2002), p. 125.

2. Ibid., p. 127.

3. Claudia L. Bushman, *America Discovers Columbus: How an Italian Explorer Became an American Hero* (Hanover, N. H.: University Press of New England, 1992), p. 41.

4. "Historical Columbia," *Wikipedia*, October 13, 2005, <http://en.wikipedia.org/wiki/Historical_Columbia> (October 15, 2005).

5. Bushman, p. 53.

6. Jonathan Eliot, *Historical Sketches of the Ten Miles Square Forming the District of Columbia* (Washington, D.C.: J. Eliot, Jr., 1830), p. 320.

7. "Tamarand," *Wikipedia*, August 28, 2005,<http://en. wikipedia.org/wiki/Tammany> (October 12, 2005).

8. Bushman, p. 82.

9. "Today in History," *The Library of Congress*, n.d., <http://memory.loc.gov/ammem/today/oct12. html> (October 12, 2005).

10. Bushman, pp. 94–95.

11. "Celebrate! Holidays in the U.S.A.—Columbus Day," *United States Embassy*, n.d., <http://www.usemb.se/ Holidays/celebrate/Columbus.html> (October 12, 2005).

12. Dennis, p. 140.
13. Matthew C. O'Conner, *Early History of the Knights of Columbus*, Handwritten manuscript (New Haven, Conn.: Knights of Columbus Archive, undated).
14. "Columbus Day," Patriotism.org, n.d., <http://www.patriotism.org/columbus_day/index.html> (October 12, 2005).
15. "Celebrate! Holidays in the U.S.A.—Columbus Day," *United States Embassy.*

❖ Chapter 4. **The Cultural Significance of Columbus Day**

1. Matthew Dennis, *Red, White, and Blue Letter Days: An American Calendar* (Ithaca, N.Y.: Cornell University Press, 2002), p. 158.
2. Claudia L. Bushman, *America Discovers Columbus: How an Italian Explorer Became an American Hero* (Hanover, N.H.: University Press of New England, 1992), pp. 102–103.
3. Ibid., pp. 100–102.
4. Ibid., p. 171.
5. "Columbus Day," *Patriotism.org*, n.d., <http://www.patriotism.org/columbus_day/index.html> (October 12, 2005).
6. "Spanish Colonization of the Americas," Wikipedia, n.d., <http://en.wikipedia.org/wiki/Spanish_colonization_of_America> (February 27, 2006).
7. Zvi Dor-Ner, *Columbus and the Age of Discovery* (New York: William Marrow and Company, 1991), p. 240.
8. Ibid., p. 240.
9. Dennis, p. 160.
10. Roger E. Hernandez, "Columbus Day is the Cultural Birthday of Hispanics," *National Minority Politics*, November 1994, vol. 6, issue 11, p. 14.

Chapter 5. Who Celebrates Columbus Day?

1. "It's Festival Time," *San Diego Business Journal,* September 27, 1999, vol. 20, issue 39, p. A2.
2. "Columbus Day," *Wikipedia,* n.d., <http://en.wiki pedia.org/wiki/Dia_de_la_Raza> (October 13, 2005).
3. Ibid.
4. Leslie Flynn, "Dia de la Raza Exalts Cultures of Latin America," October 12, 2004, <http://www.dailytexa nonline.com/media/paper410/news/2004/10/12. html> (February 27, 2005).
5. Ibid.
6. Ibid.

Chapter 6. Symbols of Columbus Day

1. "About Columbus: Santa Maria, Inc.," *The Santa Maria,* n.d., <http://www.santamaria.org> (October 13, 2005).
2. "Italian Renaissance Clothing: 1420–1520," Twin Groves School District, August 23, 2004, <http:// www.twingroves.district96.k12.il.us/Renaissance/ Town/Clothing/ClothingItalian.html> (October 13, 2005).

Chapter 7. Columbus Day Today

1. "Columbus Day," *Holiday Insights,* n.d., <http:// www.holidayinsights.com/other/columbus.htm> (October 13, 2005).
2. Claudia L. Bushman, *American Discovers Columbus: How an Italian Explorer Became and American Hero* (Hanover, N. H.: University Press of New England, 1991), p. 184.
3. Henry B. Carrington, ed. *Columbian Selections: American Patriotism, For Home and School* (Phila-delphia: J. B. Lippincott Company, 1892), pp. 32–24.

4. Gabrielle Tayac, "Interview with Rayna Green," *Northeast Indian Quarterly*, Fall 1990, vol 7, issue 3, pp. 12–13.

5. Gerald P. Fogarty, "1892 and 1992: From Celebration of Discovery to Encounter of Cultures," *Catholic Historical Review*, October 1993, vol. 79, issue 4, p. 650.

6. William Loren Katz, "Columbus and the American Holocaust," *New York Amsterdam News*, October 9, 2003, vol. 94, issue 41, p. 13.

7. Ibid., p. 13.

8. "Columbus Day," *Holiday Insights*.

9. Matthew Dennis, *Red, White, and Blue Letter Days: An American Calendar* (Ithaca N.Y.: Cornell University Press, 2002), p. 157.

10. Ibid., p. 158.

11. Christian T. Iosso, "In Columbus and in Christ: An Italian-American Presbyterian Perspective on the Quincentenary," *Network News*, September/October 1992, vol. 12, issue 5, p. 6.

12. "Columbus Day," *Holiday Insights*.

13. Iosso, p. 7.

14. Fogarty, p. 650.

FURTHER READING

Aller, Susan Bivin. *Christopher Columbus*. Minneapolis, Minn.: Lerner Publications Co., 2003.

Blue, Rose, and Corinne J. Naden. *Exploring Central America, Mexico, and the Caribbean.* Chicago: Raintree, 2004.

Gallagher, Carole S. *Christopher Columbus and the Discovery of the New World.* Philadelphia, Penn.: Chelsea House Publishers, 2000.

Sundel, Al. *Christopher Columbus and the Age of Exploration in World History.* Berkeley Heights, N.J.: Enslow Publishers, Inc., 2002.

INTERNET ADDRESSES

Age of Exploration: Christopher Columbus
   <http://www.mariner.org/educationalad/
   ageofex/columbus.php>
Read more about Christopher Columbus.

Día de la Raza: Day of the Race
   <http://www.elbalero.gob.mx/kids/about/
   html/holidays/race_kids.html>
Learn about Día de la Raza.

INDEX

8-08